This Walker book belongs to:

. . . .

. . . .

. . . .

For Gloria Molinaroli, her cat Homer
and the St Johnsbury Athenaeum
R. L.

For Polydor
A. W.

First published 2011 by Walker Books Ltd
87 Vauxhall Walk, London SE11 5HJ

This paperback edition published 2012

2 4 6 8 10 9 7 5 3

Text copyright © 2011 Reeve Lindbergh
Illustrations copyright © 2011 Anne Wilsdorf

The right of Reeve Lindbergh and Anne Wilsdorf to be identified as
author and illustrator respectively of this work has been asserted by them
in accordance with the Copyright, Designs and Patents Act 1988

This book has been typeset in Mrs Eaves

Printed in China

British Library Cataloguing in Pubication Data:
a catalogue record for this book is available from the British Library

ISBN 978-1-4063-3858-4

www.walker.co.uk

HOMER
THE LIBRARY CAT

REEVE LINDBERGH

ILLUSTRATED BY ANNE WILSDORF

WALKER BOOKS
AND SUBSIDIARIES

LONDON · BOSTON · SYDNEY · AUCKLAND

Homer was a quiet cat,
quiet as a mouse.
A quiet lady lived with him
in a quiet house.

The lady went away each day.
Homer stayed at home.
He sat beside the window,
peaceful, all alone.

He played with wool and feathers.

They made no noise at all.

When he heard a bird, he purred.

Mice played with his ball.

One morning Homer heard a CRASH
– a really awful din!
And jumping from the window
he landed in the bin.

The dustbins fell and BANGED and rolled,

and Homer ran away.

Where was the quiet lady?

What a noisy day!

The post office was just next door;
Homer went inside.
But Hope and Noah sneezed so loud
that Homer had to hide.

Inside the fire station,
he found a quiet place
just beneath the ladder,
a cosy, cat-size space.

CLANG! CLANG! The fire bell rang.

A fire! A fire in town!

Five fit firemen rushed straight out.

One quick cat jumped down.

Homer ran and ran and ran
down to the railway track.
He found an empty goods van
and jumped up in the back.

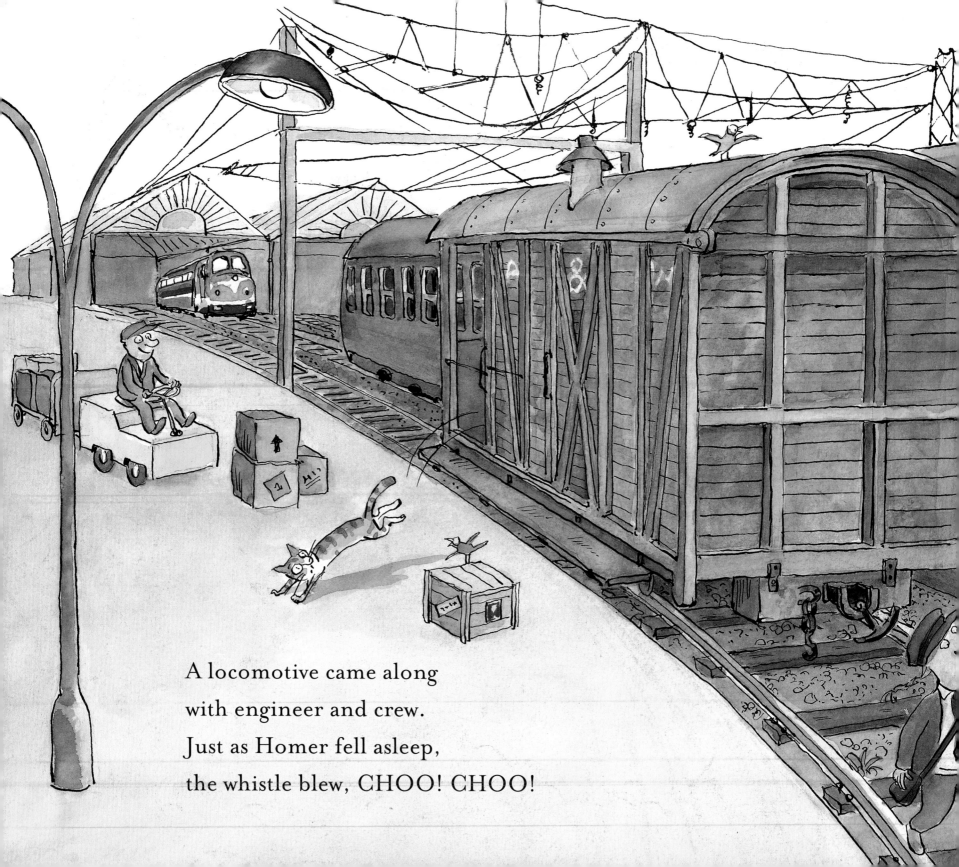

A locomotive came along
with engineer and crew.
Just as Homer fell asleep,
the whistle blew, CHOO! CHOO!

Homer ran back into town
and through an open door,
into a big bright building,
across a marble floor.

He heard a friendly voice he knew.

He saw a rocking chair.

There was the quiet lady!

And children everywhere.

"Homer!" said the lady.
"What are you doing here?"
Homer jumped into her arms
and purred into her ear.

The boys and girls loved Homer.
Homer loved them back.
He slept right through the stories
but woke up for the snack.

Now Homer is a Library Cat —
he goes there every day.
What do the children think of that?
"It's purr-fect!" they all say.

Author Reeve Lindbergh, the daughter of aviator Charles Lindbergh and Anne Morrow Lindbergh, has written many children's books, including *Nobody Owns the Sky* and *My Little Grandmother Often Forgets*, as well as novels and memoirs for adults. She lives in the USA, in Vermont.

Illustrator Anne Wilsdorf was born in Angola.
The illustrator of many books for children, she lives in Lausanne, Switzerland, where she teaches illustration.

www.walker.co.uk